P

O ==== H ==== O

Bee
Tree

Big
Stones
and rox

My House

D1058900

First American Edition.
Copyright © 1999 Disney Enterprises, Inc.
All rights reserved under international copyright
conventions. Published in the United States by Grolier
Books, a division of Grolier Enterprises Inc. Originally
published in Denmark by Egmont Gruppen, Copenhagen.

ISBN: 0-7172-8966-4

Manufactured in the United States of America.
A B C D   1 2 3 4

Based on the Pooh Stories by A.A. Milne. (copyright the
Pooh Properties Trust)

WALT DISNEY'S

Winnie the Pooh
and
Tigger Too

GROLIER
BOOKS

One sunny morning in the Hundred-Acre
Wood, Tigger was bouncing through the forest.
Boing! Boing! Boing! Boing!
"HOO-HOO-HOO!" he cried happily. "It's a
Tiggerific day for bouncin'! I think I'll drop in on
my ol' pals!"

Meanwhile, a little bear named Winnie the Pooh was busy thinking.

"Think, think, think," the bear of little brain said, trying hard to remember what he was thinking about.

Then—

WHUMP-BUMP-BUMP!

Winnie the Pooh was bounced to the ground!

"Hello, Pooh! I'm Tigger! T-I-double-Guh-Rrr! That spells Tigger!"

"Yes, I know," Pooh replied. "You've bounced me before."

"Oh. Sorry, pal," apologized Tigger. "Well, gotta go. I've got a lot of bouncin' to do. T-T-F-N. Ta-ta for now!"

And quick as a spring, Tigger bounded off.

That was Tigger. He was *always* bouncing in on his friends when they least expected it. Tigger's next stop was Piglet's house. And Piglet certainly wasn't expecting to be—

WHUMP-BUMP-BUMP!

—bounced to the ground.

"Oh, T-T-Tigger," Piglet nervously stuttered. "You s-s-scared me."

"Scared you?" Tigger said. "That was just one of my *little* bounces."

"It was?" asked Piglet, thinking that the bounce had felt awfully big to him.

"I'm saving my *best* bounce for old Long Ears," Tigger replied. "HOO-HOO-HOO-HOO! Ta-ta!"

Meanwhile, Rabbit was busy
tending his garden.

"There now," Rabbit happily
announced. "Everything's per-
fect. Carrots, lettuce, and pump-
kins, all neat and tidy."

But not for long, because just
then—

"Oh, no! No!" Rabbit cried frantically. *"Stop!"*
WHUMP-BUMP-BUMP!

Too late! Rabbit received Tigger's biggest bounce
ever. The two rolled and rolled and tumbled through
Rabbit's garden. Everything was flattened.

"Hello, Rabbit! I'm Tigger! T-I-double—"

"Oh, please!" Rabbit angrily interrupted.
"Don't spell it! Oh, dear! Just look at my garden!"

"Yuck!" Tigger said. "Kinda messy, isn't it?"

"Messy? *Messy?!* It's ruined!" moaned Rabbit.
"Oh, Tigger, why don't you *ever* stop bouncing?"

" 'Cause bouncin' is what tiggers do best!"
he answered.

Later, Pooh and Piglet went to Rabbit's house for a special Tigger protest meeting.

"Order! Order!" called Rabbit. "Tigger is getting too bouncy. It's time we taught him a lesson."

"Perhaps we should find a way to *un*bounce him," suggested Piglet.

"Yes, I agree," Rabbit replied. "What do you think, Pooh? *Pooh?* Are you listening?"

"Of course," Pooh replied, waking from a sound sleep. "But there was some fluff in my ear. Could you repeat that, please?"

"Which part?" asked Rabbit.

"The part that I didn't hear, of course," answered Pooh.

"Pooh," whispered Piglet. "We're trying to take the bounce out of Tigger."

"Oh, I've got a splendid idea!" Rabbit suddenly announced. "We'll take Tigger somewhere he's never been before. Then we'll lose him there!"

"Lose him?" asked Pooh.

"Oh, don't worry," Rabbit explained. "We'll find him again the next morning. Mark my words, it'll take the bounce *right* out of him!"

So it was agreed that they would start out the
next day. That morning turned out to be a cold and
misty one in the Hundred-Acre Wood.

The mist was so thick that the four friends
could barely see the ground in front of them.
But that didn't slow down Tigger.

Boing! Boing! Boing!

He sprang ahead into the lead.

Tigger leaped farther and farther and
deeper and deeper into the woods. Rabbit
thought it was a good time to lose him.

"Now's our chance," he said to Pooh
and Piglet. "Quick! Over here. Hide!"

Rabbit led the two friends inside an old
hollow log. Tigger soon realized his friends
were no longer behind him.

"Hey! That's
funny!" Tigger said.
"They must be lost!"

"Halloo!" Tigger called, bouncing back to look for his missing friends. "Hey, guys, where are you? *Halloo!*"

Then Tigger climbed on top of the very place where Pooh, Piglet, and Rabbit were hiding.

"HALLOO!" he shouted into the log as loud as he could.

The hidden friends' ears rang from the noise, but they said nothing.

Tigger soon gave up and *boinged* off in search of his pals. Rabbit cautiously peered out of the log.

"Hooray!" cheered Rabbit. "My splendid idea worked! Come on, let's head for home."

Rabbit was certain that everything was working according to plan. But soon the plan *stopped* working.

Pooh, Piglet, and Rabbit walked and walked and walked through the woods. But they didn't seem to be getting anywhere.

"It's funny how everything seems the same in the mist," Rabbit said. "This looks just like the sand pit where we started."

And so they tried again, but they ended up right back at the very same pit. Pooh was getting tired. He suspected the sand pit was following them. But the truth was they were lost. They had been walking around in a big circle.

"Oh, Rabbit," Pooh suggested. "How would it be if as soon as we're out of sight of this old pit, we just try to find it again?"

"Why?" asked Rabbit.

"We keep looking for home, but we keep finding this pit," Pooh explained. "So, I thought if we kept looking for this pit, maybe we'd find home."

"I don't see much sense in that," Rabbit replied.
"If I walked away from this pit, then walked back to
it, of course I'd find it. I'll prove it to you. Wait here."

So Pooh and Piglet waited in the misty sand pit
for Rabbit.

And they waited ...

... and waited ...

... and waited.

The two tired
friends fell asleep.
All the while, Pooh
dreamed of his honey
pots at home.

Grr! A strange noise startled Piglet!

"W-w-what was that, Pooh?" he asked, waking up.

"My tummy," Pooh explained. "It rumbled. I'm hungry, Piglet. Let's go home now."

"Do you know the way?" asked Piglet.

"No," answered Pooh. "But there are twelve pots of honey in my cupboard, and they have been calling to my tummy."

"They have?"

"Yes, Piglet. I couldn't hear them before because Rabbit was talking. I think I know where they're calling from," Pooh said, helping Piglet out of the sand pit. "Come on. We'll just follow my tummy."

Pooh and Piglet walked off together into the mist.
For a long time, Piglet said nothing because he did
not want to interrupt the voices of Pooh's honey pots.
Sure enough, the mist soon got thinner and Piglet
began to know where he was. When suddenly—

"HOO-HOO-HOO-HOO!"
It was Tigger!
WHUMP-BUMP-BUMP!
He bounced Pooh and Piglet to the ground.

"Hello there, you two!" Tigger cried.
"Where have you been?"

"We've been trying to find our way back
home," explained Pooh.

"Say, where's old Long Ears?" asked Tigger.

"He must still be missing in the mist," Pooh said.

"Well, leave it to me," Tigger declared.
"I'll go and bounce him right out of there!
T-T-F-N—ta-ta for now!"

So Tigger romped off to find Rabbit. Meanwhile, Rabbit was still wandering around in the cold mist. By now he was most definitely lost and certainly scared.

His frightened mind played tricks on him. Rabbit
began to hear noises … strange noises … *scary* noises!

CHOMP-CHOMP!
"Pooh? Piglet? Is that y-you?"
KRUNCH!
"*Aaagghh!*" yelled Rabbit.

CROAK!
"What was that?!"
Rabbit cried fearfully.
BR-RIBBIT!
"W-who's there?"

"Help!" Rabbit screamed, running off
in an awful panic!
Who should he bump into but—
WHUMP-BUMP-BUMP!

"Hello, Rabbit!"

"Tigger!" the bounced bunny cried in surprise. "B-but you're supposed to be lost!"

"Lost? Tiggers *never* get lost, buddy boy!" Tigger cheerfully replied.

"Never?" Rabbit asked sadly. He realized that his splendid plan had not worked at all.

"Of course not!" Tigger said. "Come on, Rabbit! Let's go home! HOO-HOO-HOO-HOO!"

So the two started back. Rabbit was not a
happy Rabbit. He was a tired Rabbit. A lost-and-
found Rabbit. A why-oh-why-do-these-things-
happen-to-me Rabbit!

But Rabbit had learned his lesson. Never again
would he try to change his friends. He was lucky to
have them just the way they were.

Nise For Piknics

Rabbits
Howse
Piglet

Sand pit
where Roo playe

Owl

Pooh Bears Howse →

MR SANDERS

100 Aker Wood

Floody Place